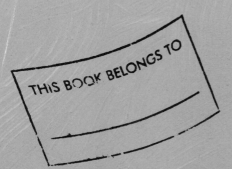

THIS BOOK BELONGS TO

_____

THIS BOOK BELONGS TO

_____

I LOVE GOING THROUGH THIS BOOK

BY ROBERT BURLEIGH
ILLUSTRATED BY DAN YACCARINO

THIS BOOK BELONGS TO

_____

JOANNA COTLER BOOKS
An Imprint of HarperCollinsPublishers

I Love Going Through This Book   Text copyright © 2001 by Robert Burleigh   Illustrations copyright © 2001 by Dan Yaccarino   Printed in Hong Kong.
All rights reserved.   www.harperchildrens.com   Library of Congress Cataloging-in-Publication Data   Burleigh, Robert.   I love going through this book
/ by Robert Burleigh; illustrated by Dan Yaccarino.   p.   cm.   Summary: For one reader, going through a book is an incredible adventure.
ISBN 0-06-028805-1—ISBN 0-06-028806-X (lib. bdg.)   [1. Books and reading—Fiction. 2. Stories in rhyme.] I. Yaccarino, Dan, ill.
II. Title. PZ8.3.B9526 lk 2001 99-88386 [E]—dc21   Typography by Alicia Mikles   1 2 3 4 5 6 7 8 9 10 ❖ First Edition

THIS BOOK BELONGS TO
_____

THIS BOOK BELONGS TO
_____

THIS BOOK BELONGS TO
_____

THIS BOOK BELONGS TO
_____

For Felix Burleigh Freeland.
May he travel through many books
and have many adventures!

—R.B.

I LOVE GOING THROUGH this book.
Just watch me do it.
No matter how long it takes,
I'm going all the way through it!

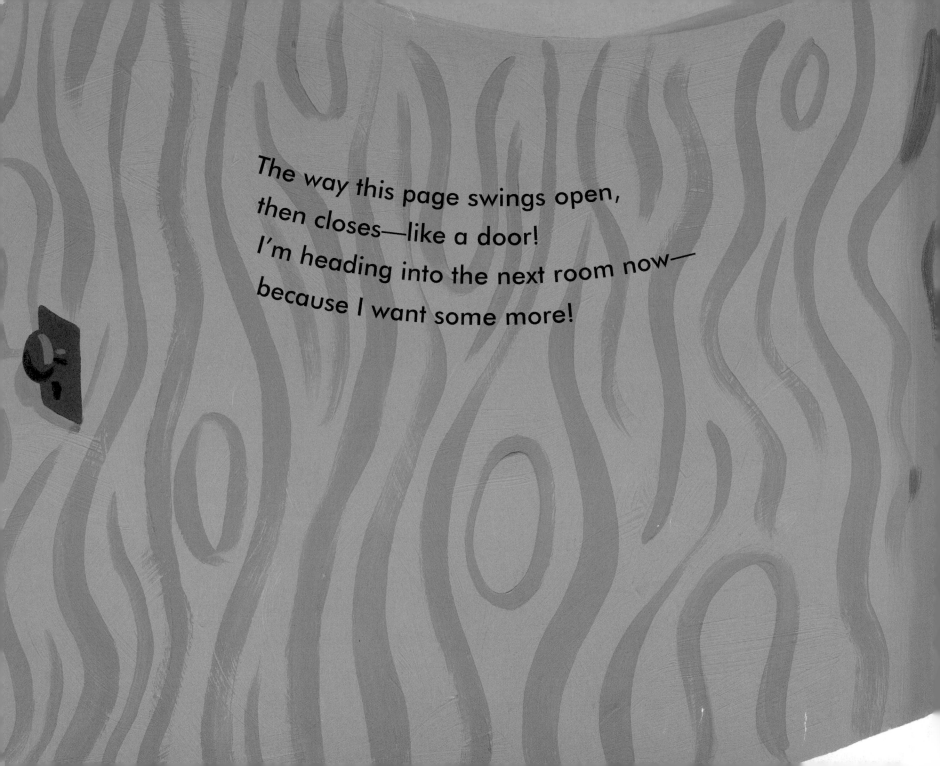

The way this page swings open,
then closes—like a door!
I'm heading into the next room now—
because I want some more!

Is this page like a wall? So what!
I'll hoist my ladder and climb.

Is this page like a meadow?
I'll stroll and take my time.

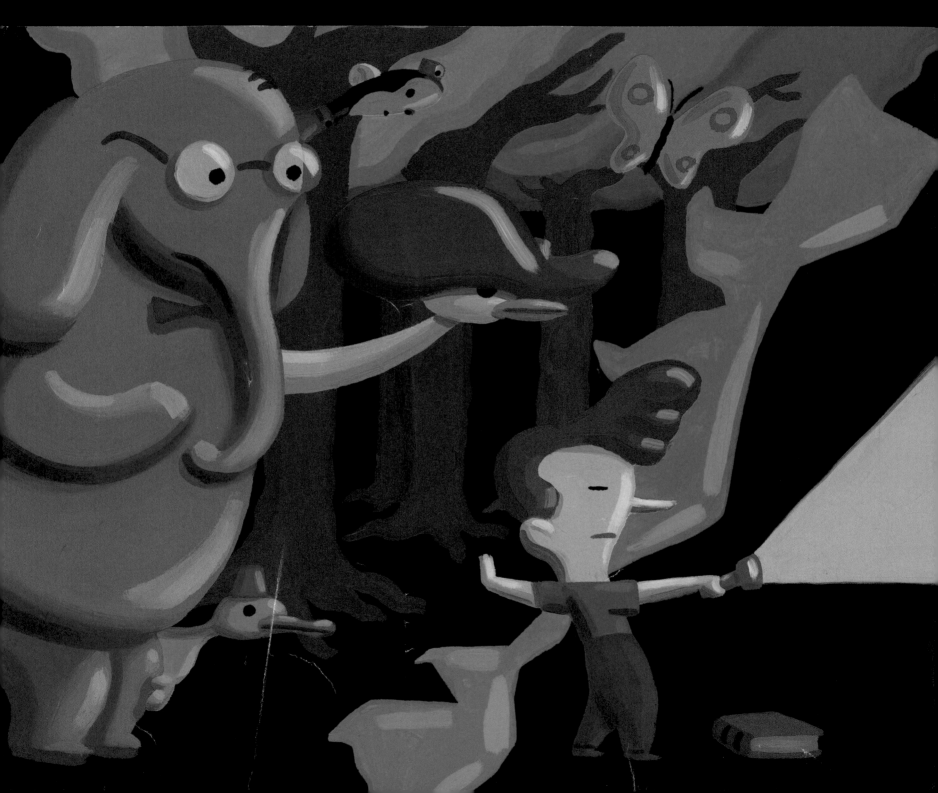

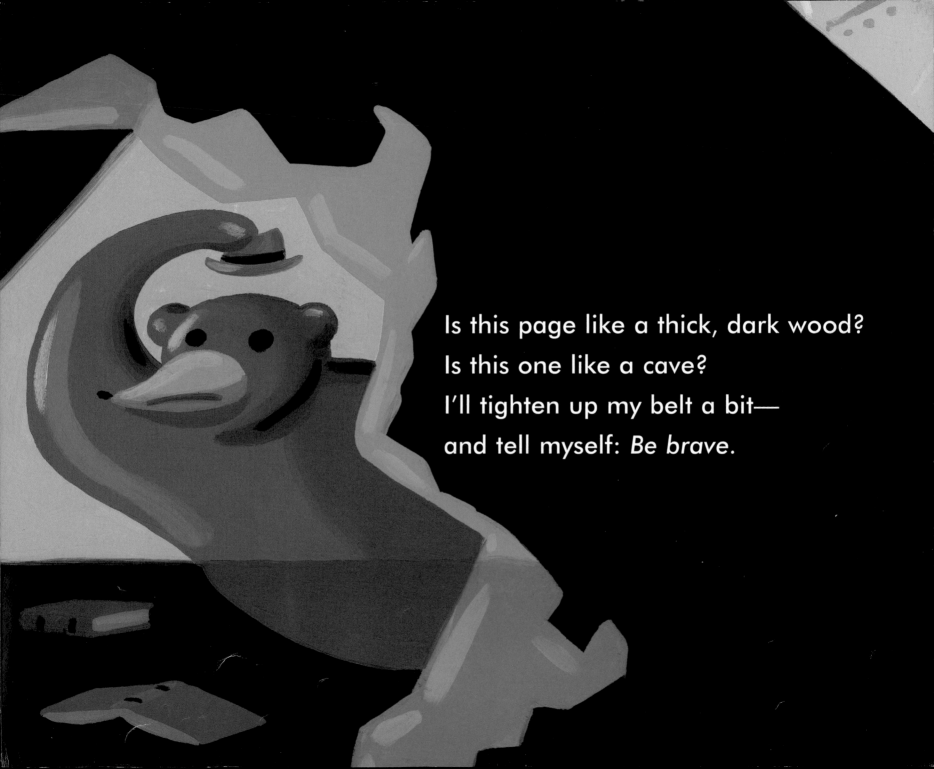

Is this page like a thick, dark wood?
Is this one like a cave?
I'll tighten up my belt a bit—
and tell myself: *Be brave.*

Where to? When? Why? What next?
That's what I want to know.

But please, don't anyone tell me.
I'll find out as I go.

I love going through this book.
I like the way it feels.
I like the fresh smell of the page,
the crunch of leaves beneath my heels.

I like to raft down wide, wide rivers
and feel the soft breeze blowing.
I like to go from summer days . . .

. . . to where it's cold and snowing.

I love to see a starry sky.
I love these strange new places.

I like the people that I meet.
I like these open spaces.

But look—around that bend!
Come on, feet, let's go!
We'll hike up to the very top
and see what's far below.

I feel the wind behind me.
I'm spinning as I slide
past mountain lakes and rocks and trees—
straight down the mountainside.

THE END

THIS BOOK BELONGS TO

THIS BOOK BELONGS TO

OOK BELONGS TO

I told you I'd do it, I told you.
And now I did it. Look:
I got through, I got through, I got through,
all the way through this book!

THE

Wait—the fun's not over yet.
I'll catch my breath—and then,
walk around to the front of the book,

THIS BOOK BELONGS TO

THIS BOOK BELONGS TO

and go back through again!